Why Are You Still Here?

Lynda Partridge

Illustrations: Dave Nicholson

T0306936

DURVILE & UpRoute Books

Calgary, Alberta, Canada

DURVILE &
UpRoute Books

Durvile & UpRoute Books
UPROUTE IMPRINT OF DURVILE PUBLICATIONS LTD.

Calgary, Alberta, Canada
DURVILE.COM

LIBRARY AND ARCHIVES CATALOGUING IN PUBLICATIONS DATA

Why Are You Still Here?: A Lillian Mystery
Partridge, Lynda, author
Nicholson, Dave, Illustrator

1. First Nations | 2. Indigenous
3. Spirit World | 4. Folklore

UpRoute Spirit of Nature Series. Series editor, Raymond Yakeleya

ISBN: 978-1-988824-82-6 (pbk)
978-1-988824-92-5 (ebook)
978-1-988824-93-2 (audiobook)

Book design, Lorene Shyba
Jacket illustrations, Dave Nicholson

Durvile Publications would like to acknowledge the financial support of the Government of Canada through Canadian Heritage Canada Book Fund and the Government of Alberta, Alberta Media Fund.

Canada Alberta Government

Printed in Canada. First edition, first printing. 2022.

We acknowledge the traditional lands upon which we live, work, and play. The Indigenous Peoples of Southern Alberta include the Siksika, Piikani, and Kainai of the Blackfoot Confederacy; the Tsuut'ina; and the Chiniki, Bearspaw, and Wesley Stoney Nakoda First Nations. Also the Region 3 Métis Nation of Alberta.

DEDICATION

This book is dedicated to all the
Indigenous children who were sent to
the Spirit World before their time.
The hope is that truth and reconciliation can
have some real meaning when the voices of
children are heard and believed.

TABLE OF CONTENTS

TABLE OF CONTENTS

Chloe found an old beat-up camera
in the office of the old barn.

Chapter 1

The Camera and the Window

GRACE SWORE there was a window in that darn old barn. Every time she looked through her cousin Chloe's old camera she saw a window. When she looked with just her eyes she didn't.

"There's nothing on the lens," she muttered, "and it's not on a weird setting." She handed the camera back to Chloe. "Look again, do you still see it?" she asked

"Holy crap. Yep, I see it too. That's just too weird."

They passed the camera back and forth, both trying to figure out how there was a light coming from a window that didn't exist in the old barn. They stared at the barn trying to see it with just their eyes, but all they saw was the dark barn board against the slowly darkening sky. They passed the camera back and forth a few more times. They looked at the barn from different angles just in case the light was reflecting somehow from the ground or the pond, or from anywhere, really.

"Your camera is awfully beat up," Grace mused. "Maybe there's something on the lens?"

When Grace asked Chloe where she had gotten the camera, Chloe had to stop and think for a minute. She remembered that she had found it while playing around in the old part of the barn that had once been an office for her family's chicken business.

"I found it on a shelf buried under a bunch of old empty egg cartons," said Chloe. They both looked over the camera again. It wasn't dirty and didn't have any cracks or anything. It looked like one of the very first digital cameras ever made. Grace pulled out her phone and used the camera setting to look at the barn instead. Nope. There was no window that time. They were starting to get goose bumps.

"Let's go in the house," Grace said, "and don't tell your mom about this. She'll think we're both eating too much sugar again. She thinks it warps our mind."

Chloe nodded and shoved the old camera into her knapsack to hide it.

Grace loved her Aunt Bernie, Chloe's mom,

but Aunt Bernie could be a real pain when it came to excessive anything and that included video games, movies, and candy. They really didn't want to lose their treats for the summer. Grace loved her Uncle Leroy too, who was her mom Sandra's brother, even though Uncle Leroy seemed more distracted and sad every summer she saw him.

It was nice and warm when they went inside. Grace thought her cousin was so lucky to live on a big ol' farm. Her house was what was called a Heritage House. The plaque on the house said it was from 1853 but Uncle Leroy said it was probably at least ten years older than that. A Heritage House meant that they couldn't do anything to change the way the outside of the house looked. Grace couldn't imagine why anyone would want to. It was a huge two-story stone house with big wooden doors and old wooden floors that creaked, and had not just one, but two staircases that lead upstairs. Grace and Chloe's bedroom took up the back part of the upper floor. The rickety old staircase from the kitchen went straight up into their room. There was a smaller room as well that was Chloe's little brother Wally's room. Mostly they just ignored him. After all, they were almost twelve and he was only eight and a royal pain in the behind as far as they were concerned.

They raced by Grace's Aunt Bernie, Chloe's mom, and ran up the rickety stairs to Chloe's room that was also Grace's room in the summer-time. It had a big bay window that faced out from the back of the house and stared straight at that barn wall where they saw the window that didn't really exist. From that vantage point they could also see the pond and the wharf at the edge of the meadow. They stared with bare eyes at the barn through the bay window, thinking this new angle might make a difference.

"Holy catfish," said Grace in amazement. "I don't see the window from here either." She turned to Chloe and asked, "How about you?"

"Me neither," whispered Chloe, totally stunned.

"'K, Chloe, give me the camera and let me look through it again." Grace felt tingles up her back and neck and across her arms. "Oh man, you're not going to believe this, Chloe. It's there again. The window and the light." She handed the camera back to Chloe.

"Okay. I'm weirding out," she said. "I see it again too. I'm gonna take some pictures and see what happens." Chloe took five pictures. When they looked at the pictures there was a fuzzy white spot in the picture but nothing like a window. They couldn't really tell what it was.

"Grace, what are we going to do?" asked Chloe.

"I don't know," Grace replied. "But let's not tell your mom yet till we figure this out. I don't want her to cut us off sweets all summer."

Chapter 2

Wally's Magic World

"GRACE, CHLOE come on down for supper now," Aunt Bernie shouted from the bottom of the old stairway. Grace and Chloe looked at each other making a silent oath to keep everything to themselves for now. "Okay, we're on our way!" they yelled at the same time.

"What should we do with the camera?" Grace asked.

"Stick it under your mattress," Chloe muttered "and let's get going."

They washed their hands in the upstairs bathroom and ran down the well-worn wooden stairs from Chloe's room that led straight into the kitchen and Aunt Bernie. "Slow down girls, before you fall and break an arm. There will be no broken anythings this year, thank you very much." The girls grinned at each other remembering last summer break when Grace fell out of the massive

Catalpa tree beside the driveway and broke her arm on the very first day of their time together.

"We'll be more careful this year, Aunt Bernie. We promise this will be a calm year. No crazy adventures. We are older and much more mature this year. Remember, we're eleven and a half now, not ten and a half like last year."

Aunt Bernie looked at them both and rolled her eyes to the back of her head. "Uh-huh," was all she said out loud. But inside her head she told herself how lucky she was that they were both on the youngish side for their age. They just loved having fun together on the farm and for the most part didn't get into too much trouble.

Aunt Bernie loved to cook and bake. She and Uncle Leroy always tried to fatten Grace up when she came for the summer. They said she looked like a scrawny little city kid who didn't get enough sun. Grace and Chloe helped set the table automatically as that was their job every meal time. They didn't have to be reminded every day, just sometimes when they got caught up in their 'adventures.'

"Oh, good grief," said Aunt Bernie. "Where's Wally now? I called for him at least 20 minutes ago. Can you please go outside and find your brother. I don't know what that boy gets up to out there."

The girls looked at each other knowingly. Wally lived in his own little world and loved making up stories about strange lands and magical people and animals. They had a pretty good idea where he was. Wally was very much like his dad. Uncle Leroy was a band member of the First Nations community down the road. Chloe took more after her mom who was non-Indigenous.

Chloe went out to get him, pretty confident she knew exactly where to find him, and she was right. She found him by the pond playing with the water, and sand, and rocks. She could hear him talking but couldn't make out what he was saying. "Wally, get in the house right now. Mom's having a meltdown 'cause you don't come in the house when you're called. We're about to sit down to supper."

Chloe loved her little brother but sometimes she just wanted him not to be her responsibility.

"I'm coming Chloe. Sorry."

"Hurry up."

As they were leaving Chloe thought she heard Wally say: "See ya later."

"Hey Wally who you talking to, your imaginary friend?" she scoffed.

Wally just shook his head and headed to the house with her.

"We're back, Mom. Wally was at the pond talking to the wild things again."

"Never mind," scolded her mom. "Wally, just hurry and go wash up. Your dad's a hungry bear waiting to eat."

Everyone enjoyed their first summer evening meal together with lots of love and laughter. After supper, both Aunt Bernie and Uncle Leroy shooed the three kids outside. "We'll clean up tonight. You three go have fun outside. Wally, make sure you feed Bertram before you go out." Bertram was hard to forget, as the crazy little bull terrier was running circles around Wally trying to get his attention.

The girls took advantage of the quiet time and just stared at the landscape from the covered porch. They could see the two acres of prime grapes just starting to look like the beautiful red wine grapes they would grow into. A little further away they could see the corn fields that Aunt Bernie and Uncle Leroy rented to a local farmer.

They loved watching the corn grow through the summer and would even sneak out to run through the fields when they thought they could get away with it. They let their imaginations run wild and made up weird and wonderful stories about what happened in those fields when no one was watching. It was night time when their stories got really wild and all sorts of supernatural, ghostly things happened. This was the main reason they didn't want to tell anyone about the window in the barn. They would just be told they were letting their imaginations run on overtime.

"Let's take a walk before we're hauled back inside at dark," Chloe suggested. Together, as though led by some unseen force, they took a left turn and headed straight for the barn. Grace and Chloe looked at each other and clasped their hands together. They ran the short distance to the front of the barn and came to a full stop. The barn was huge — humongous, in fact. The two end parts looked like possessed arms that were either welcoming or threatening them. They couldn't decide.

"Jeez, Grace, I'm getting kinda weird feelings," Chloe stuttered. "Maybe we should wait till daylight before going in there again. This twilight is weird. Everything is weird. There's no other word to describe it. I don't remember anything happening like this before." They scanned the outside of the barn from one side to the other. Neither of them saw anything different but they sure felt it. What they didn't see was a window anywhere. They walked all the way around the outside and they still didn't see anything. "Chloe, let's go back to the house now," Grace whispered, not really sure why. "I think too much is happening too fast. Let's go back and forget about the camera and window till tomorrow."

They ran back to the porch and had to stop to catch their breath.

"Remember not a word to anyone, especially Wally," Chloe warned. "He'll go straight to my mom. Where is he anyway?"

They looked out in the fields and saw him running through the grapes with Bertram. "Girls, go find Wally. It's time to come in for the night," Aunt Bernie yelled from somewhere inside.

They ran out into the field and Bertram came bounding towards them. He loved having someone extra around to give him more attention. "Come on, Wally!" screamed Chloe. "In the house now." Walter gave the 'just a minute' signal with his hand. "Now, Wally, or you deal with mom's curfew tomorrow!" At that, Wally zipped across the grape patch and they walked back to the house wrapped in their own thoughts.

When they got inside both Aunt Bernie and Uncle Leroy gave them all big hugs and sent them off to get ready for bed. It had been a long day and the beginning of loads of time they'd have together.

Wally usually went to bed before the girls but tonight all three were exhausted so they headed to their beds at the same time. Grace and Chloe thought they would stay awake all night talking, but instead they were already snuggling into their pillows. As Chloe was falling asleep she mumbled to Grace. "Hey, remind me to tell you about Lillian tomorrow. She's a new kid I met. She's really cool and you'll like her…and…." The next minute they were both asleep.

Chapter 3

Another Guest at the Farm

It took Grace a minute to remember where she was but the smell of bacon and eggs sure made her brain wake up. Usually, they only had toast or cereal for breakfast back in the city. Suddenly she remembered the camera under her mattress and pulled it out to look at the pictures again. You still couldn't figure out what the fuzzy white spot was. She looked out the window and just saw the regular old barn. She got brave and looked through the view finder and there it was again — the window. But no light this time.

"Wake up, Chloe. Come on noodle head, wake up."

Grace not-so-gently prodded Chloe's feet, which hung over the edge of the bed. Chloe jumped straight up in the air with a blood curdling scream: "Let me go you slimy green-haired monster, let me go!" Grace grabbed her sides from laughing so hard. Slowly, Chloe woke up for real and when she got her bearings she glared at Grace. “Not funny,” she said.

“Heck yeah, it was. I almost peed myself! You’re hilarious.”

“Someone better be dying up there, or have a darned good reason for that noise!”

“Sorry, Aunt Bernie! It won’t happen again.”

And with that, summer started at the farm.

As soon as the special breakfast was over they were reminded that as of this day it was back to regular routines. The girls were fidgety, wanting to get outside and check out the barn with the camera. As soon as they finished helping with breakfast cleanup, they tore out the door and ran to the barn. Of course, they couldn’t see a window because they’d forgotten the camera and were too lazy to go back into the house. Instead they wandered all around the barn looking for anything unusual, but saw nothing. They went into the chicken coop to watch the hens for a while then checked the old office where Chloe had found the camera.

Suddenly, Bertram came running into the old office with his hackles up and barked at the shelves.

"Quiet!" they yelled at the same time but he only looked at them for a second before he continued barking, keeping his gaze on the wall.

"Maybe it's a mouse," Grace suggested. They both got weirded out, grabbed Bertram's collar and hauled him out of the office with them. They decided to forget about the barn and for the whole day they just goofed around outside.

It was almost suppertime before Chloe remembered she was going to tell Grace about her new friend Lillian.

"Hey cuz," she said. "You're going to get to meet a new friend I made this year. She visits her Kokum down the road at the Rez where my dad is from. Her name is Lillian and she spends lots of time here, and I spend lots of time there. Mom and Lillian's Kokum are good friends and do lots of community stuff together. She's super cool. You'll get to meet her soon."

"Sounds good," Grace replied. "I'm sure I'll like her if you do. Does that mean your dad's visiting his family more? I thought you didn't have much to do with them."

"Mom and I do, just Dad not so much. Lillian's Kokum has been spending time talking with him though, so he's coming around. Anyway, I go to the Rez lots 'cause my mom says it's my right to know that side of my culture. Even though Mom is non-Indigenous she says I am, and I need to know who I am. Me and Lillian have that in common. Her dad was non-Indigenous and my mom is non-Indigenous." Chloe and Grace looked at each other, wrapped up in their personal thoughts about family and culture. They smiled at each other knowing that no matter what, they would always be family and best friends. They would always have crazy fun adventures together. "Okay, let's get inside before Mom sends out the search party."

After supper, Wally and the girls watched TV for half an hour before getting ready for bed. As they were heading upstairs, though, they were called into the kitchen for a family meeting.

"Okay kids," Aunt Bernie said. "We have a situation that requires everyone's input. As you are well aware, there has been a pretty severe outbreak of flu on the Rez. The flu and the recent flooding have caused quite a few problems for people living there. The community leaders have reached out and asked for some help for the young and the Elders who have been the most effected. I know you've been upset with having to stay on the farm and not being able to visit your family but we really don't want to run the risk of you getting sick.

"Grace, your mom and I decided it would be good for Wally and Chloe to have some family time with you. That's why, this summer, you came a little earlier than you usually do. Chloe, your friend Lillian's Auntie is answering the call for help and she is coming down to help. So, long story short, she doesn't want Lillian staying with her Kokum as this flu seems to be affecting children and older people the worst. They've asked if Lillian can stay here while they help with the sick and those who need help with cleaning up from the floods. Lillian's Kokum wondered if...

"Wahoo!" yelled Chloe, "Oh man! We're going to have a blast, Grace!"

"Well," Aunt Bernie continued. "I didn't get to finish my sentence and ask how you felt about her staying here, but I see that's okay with you. You okay with it too, Wally?"

"Yeah," he replied. "I really like Lillian, she gets me."

"Okay, it's settled then. She arrives tomorrow. We'll set an extra bed up in your room, girls. Thanks, all three of you, for being so generous of heart. Now, off to bed everyone! Big day tomorrow."

They all ran off to bed including Bertram who jumped into bed with Wally.

"Hey Grace," Chloe whispered. "Get that camera from under your bed. I wanna look again." The girls stared at the barn, but they saw nothing unusual. Then, they each looked through the camera viewfinder and saw the window in the barn once again. They quickly shut the curtains and decided they were both seeing things and decided to forget about it till morning. "G'night," they said to each other, and fell asleep trying not to think about the window in the barn.

Chapter 4

Lillian Arrives

"Rise and shine kids, big day ahead!" Aunt Bernie yelled up the stairs. "Come get breakfast. We have lots of work to do."

Wally, already up and dressed long ago, dashed ahead of Grace and Chloe, with Bertram nipping at his heels. The girls stumbled along as they tried to shake the cobwebs out of their brains.

Once breakfast was over, all three kids plus one dog gathered in the living room with Aunt Bernie and Uncle Leroy. "Okay girls," Aunt Bernie said. "You can go on out to the truck to help carry Lillian's bed into the house. Lillian's Auntie sent it over. Wally you can go into the linen closet upstairs and find some nice sheets and towels. Lillian and her Kokum will be for lunch."

The camera and window were forgotten while the girls helped wrestle Lillian's bed up the stairs. All three kids helped set up the bedroom to accommodate Lillian for the summer. Wally was secretly very happy Lillian was staying with them because she was always super nice to him and took the time to talk with him. Right after rearranging the room, they all went outside to pass the time until Lillian arrived.

Around noon they heard the truck coming up the driveway and they all ran towards the house, with Bertram barking loudly as he bounded ahead. The truck barely came to a stop before Lillian jumped out and ran towards Chloe. "Hey Chloe, I'm back!" she yelled. "I'm here for the whole summer and I get to stay at your house and it's super cool and — oh." Lillian stopped short when she saw Wally and Grace. "Hey Wally, *Kwey, Anin tash epideg*?"

"*Kwey* things are going good thanks," Wally replied.

Then Lillian noticed Grace. "Hey, Hi, I'm Lillian."

"Hi, I'm Grace."

"Sorry guys," Chloe chimed in. "Lillian, this is my cousin Grace I told you about from the city. You haven't met her till now 'cause every time you guys were here you were always here at different times." They grinned at each other

Auntie, Kokum, and Lillian arrive at the farm.

shyly. "Anyway we're gonna have a blast together this year. We have to stick around the farm cause my parents are super cautious, but I think we'll be busy this summer anyway."

Lillian smiled and walked back to the adults. She grabbed one hand each of both her Kokum and Auntie and led the two women towards Grace. "This is my Auntie and Kokum," Lillian beamed.

"Hi Grace," Auntie and Kokum said at the same time, smiling at her. "So happy to finally meet you. Thank you for sharing your summer home with Lillian."

"*Kwe* Chloe, *Kwe* Wally," they said. "*Miigwech* to you two as well for sharing your home with Lillian. She has been looking forward to this day."

The adults watched the interactions and smiled, knowing that all four kids were going to be just fine together.

"Okay everyone," announced Aunt Bernie. "Inside for lunch. You can help Lillian take her stuff upstairs after you eat."

Lunch was over quickly and soon all four kids were hauling suitcases and boxes upstairs. "Kokum sent some sweetgrass for us all to put in our bedrooms," stated Lillian. "She also sent some Indian tobacco for you, Wally, to put out in the woods when you're talking with your friends."

Chloe and Grace looked at each other with a surprised expression. They were surprised that Lillian knew about his weird talks to non-existent things and they were equally surprised she thought it was okay and normal. Wally smiled as he took the tobacco and went to put it in his abalone shell on his shelf in his room.

Lillian continued chatting as though nothing unusual was happening. "I saw the look you gave Grace, Chloe," she said. "Just because you have been ignoring the old ways doesn't mean they don't exist. Someday maybe your Kokum will teach you as much as my Kokum and Auntie taught me. Stop picking on your brother. He is special and has some gifts not given to everyone."

The girls hung their heads, sorry for having caused unhappiness. "'K," Lillian said "it's over and we're on to a new day of being good and thoughtful to each other. Let's have fun now."

All three laughed and giggled for the rest of the afternoon while they made Lillian a nice and comfy private space in the girls' room. Lillian put her stuffed Blue Bear on her bed and looked around. "Thanks, everyone," she said. "I feel like this is home for the next while."

“I like your bear.” Grace smiled.

“He is a special bear. I’ll tell you his story another time.” Lillian smiled to herself when she looked at her bear. Being a foster kid had been very hard on her until she came to be in the home of Auntie who was Indigenous. After having been in so many different non-Indigenous foster homes that didn’t understand her and experiencing things a child shouldn’t have to, she had been pleasantly surprised to find an adult in her life who understood her and helped her to learn about her Indigenous self. She had finally experienced love, and Auntie’s mother, now Lillian’s Kokum, whom she also called Kokomis, had also helped Lillian feel accepted. The blue bear was part of a story Kokum told her to help her feel she belonged. It had also helped her cope with the loss of her baby sister. No one seemed to know where her sister was and Auntie had tried to find out from Lillian’s social worker but even she hadn’t been able to help. *Yep, definitely a story to tell Grace and Chloe another time,* Lillian thought to herself.

Chapter 5

Keeping Secrets

"COME ON DOWNSTAIRS NOW KIDS," Aunt Bernie said. "Lillian's Aunt and Kokum are leaving. They won't be back for a while once they start working in their community."

All four went racing down the stairs followed closely by Bertram. Bertram couldn't believe he had all these little humans to keep him company.

Everyone gathered around the huge table that sat in the middle of the big kitchen. They shared supper while everyone talked about how life would be for the next while. Lillian was sad that she wouldn't be seeing her Kokum and Auntie for a while but she understood the important work they were doing in her community. They discussed how they would keep in touch everyday through texting and video chats. Everyone hugged as they all knew it would be a while before they could hug again. Kokum burnt some tobacco

Lillian with Kokomis and Auntie.
Every year, there is a pow wow on the Rez
where they dance and enjoy cultural events.

and sage and said a prayer thanking the Creator for providing a safe home, and thanking friends and family for helping. The four kids went outside after saying their goodbyes and ran off to the barn leaving the adults to talk about adult things.

Wally went to the pond with Bertram while the three girls circled the barn slowly. Grace and Chloe looked at each other and gave a little nod. "You tell her, Chloe," said Grace. "Tell me what?" quizzed Lillian.

"There's something weird happening in the barn," Chloe said. "I have an old camera I found and when I look through the viewfinder I can see a window up there."

Lillian looked to where she was pointing but she saw only barnboard. "I don't see any window." "Yeah I know," replied Chloe. "That's the problem and that's what's weird. You can only see it through the viewfinder."

Grace was quick to explain, "We'll show you when we get back to our bedroom. We forgot to bring the camera with us."

Chloe added, "When Bertram comes here with us he goes all weird too. He keeps looking up at the hay loft and barking and growling as if he sees something."

Lillian nodded thoughtfully and asked, "Chloe, what does your mom think it is?"

"We haven't told her," Chloe said. "She'll just think we've had too much sugar and that our imaginations have run to the crazy side."

"Hmm," mused Lillian.

"Let's find Wally and head back to the house," suggested Grace. "It's getting dark."

The girls walked towards the pond shouting Wally's name. Bertram came bounding from around the barn closely followed by Wally and they returned to the house together. When they got back, Lillian's Auntie and Kokum had left. They went inside and talked with Aunt Bernie and Uncle Leroy for a while then said goodnight and went upstairs.

The girls huddled together in front of the bay window facing the barn. Grace went and grabbed the camera from under her mattress. "'K, Lillian, what do you see when you look at the barn?"

Lillian answered, "Barnboard, a big wall… nothing special."

Grace replied, "Now look through the lens

Lillian, Chloe, and Grace realize they have a mystery to solve.

of this camera. what do you see?"

Although it was already quite dark, Lillian took the camera and looked through the viewfinder. She squinted her eyes, took the camera away from her eye, put it back and looked again. "Oh no," she said. "No, no, something is wrong here. How can this be?"

Grace and Chloe looked at her wide-eyed, then they looked at each other, and finally back at Lillian. "What'd we tell you, huh?" Chloe whispered. "It's kinda creepy, but I dunno something's going on…I think we have a mystery adventure ahead of us this summer."

Lillian nodded. "Tomorrow we'll go to the barn and explore," she said. "Tonight, let's get lots of sleep. I think this mystery will take up all our energy."

"Remember, not a word to my parents or Wally," Chloe added.

The other two girls nodded. The three girls got into bed and yelled "Good night Wally and Bertram!" in unison so he'd hear them from his room.

"G'night," he mumbled back, as he'd already been half asleep.

They could hear Aunt Bernie coming up

the back steps to say goodnight. She popped her head in their room to say goodnight and reminded them to be quiet and save their energy for the next day. She looked in on Wally, but he was already asleep. Smiling, she went back downstairs knowing the kids were all in a good place.

Grace, Lillian, and Chloe wonder why the window is only visible in the viewfinder.

Chapter 6

A Blurry White Light

THE NEXT MORNING after breakfast, Grace, Chloe, and Lillian headed straight to the barn, with the camera tucked into Grace's knapsack. Wally stayed behind to hang out with his mom for a while. His dad was going to let him help with the farm chores that day, which was something Wally loved to do.

The three girls slowed up as they got closer to the barn. Lillian looked around to see if there was anything different in the barnboard but she couldn't see anything.

Do you guys see anything right now?" Lillian asked.

"Nope," said Grace and Chloe together.

"Okay, haul out the camera then and let's all look before we go in the barn," said Lillian. Each of them took a turn looking through the viewfinder and they all saw the same thing — a full-size window that was as big as a picture window in a house. They tried to see into the area behind it, but all they saw was a very blurry white light.

"Let's go inside the barn and see what we feel," suggested Lillian.

"Sounds good," replied Grace.

"I'm in too," added Chloe. They walked into the old office area first and stood still, listening and trying to see if there was anything weird or different but none of them saw or felt anything. "This is where Bertram went really weird last time we were here," said Chloe. "Wish he was here now."

They left the old office and walked towards the other end of the barn where the chickens were. Other than a lot of loud clucking and scurrying they didn't notice anything strange.

"Okay," Chloe said. "This time we'll go up in the loft. It goes the whole way across this huge barn. It's full of hay and straw so be careful. We're not really supposed to go up there but I think we have to."

Chloe led the way followed by Grace then Lillian. When they got to the top, they looked all around but none of them saw anything unusual — and certainly not a window.

"Well, maybe we are just imagining things," suggested Chloe " I don't see anything different or creepy."

Grace asked, "How about we just go and goof off till suppertime?"

"Good plan. I dunno, I feel a little weird up here," said Lillian "Let's get outta here."

The girls scrambled carefully down the stairs but all three of them failed to notice the indentation of two footsteps in the straw pointed in their direction.

"We may as well collect some eggs while we're here and take them up to the house. That will put us in the good books for some junk food," Chloe quipped. "My mom will be happy we took the initiative." She emphasized the word 'initiative' knowing her mom would praise their effort with exactly that word. They all laughed knowing it was probably true. Chloe continued, "The egg aprons are hanging over there. You two can put them on to carry the eggs, and I'll collect them."

Lillian went to get the apron to put on and stopped dead in her tracks. She noticed something in the corner of her eye but when she turned to figure out what it was she saw nothing. She thought she heard a 'swoosh' sound and she snapped her head around quickly. Again, she saw something fleetingly out of the corner of her eye. Once more she saw nothing. The little hairs on the back of her neck stood up.

"What the heck," she muttered. "That sort of thing only happens in scary stories and movies." Lillian glanced over at the other two but they were chattering to each other like nothing different was going on.

"Whoever you are, stop," Lillian said to the space behind her. "Or tell me what you want." Goose bumps started down her arms. She gave the air a stare and shook her head. Maybe she was just getting carried away by Chloe and Grace's stories. Lillian ran over and joined the other two to help collect the eggs. Once they had collected all the eggs they could find, they left the barn and went up to the house for lunch.

Chapter 7

Footprints

When the three girls got back to the house, Aunt Bernie was the only one there. Uncle Leroy and Wally were out in the fields and they had taken their lunch with them.

"We brought the eggs up," announced Chloe as they arrived.

"Way to go girls!" replied her mom. "Great initiative."

The three girls looked at each other and giggled. "What's so funny?" asked Aunt Bernie.

"Nothing," they wheezed.

"Okay, well, give me a few minutes and I'll make you three some lunch. Put the eggs in the fridge and go find something to do."

After putting the eggs away the girls ran up the back stairs to take another look at the barn. Once again, Chloe and Grace didn't see anything, but Lillian did. When Lillian looked this time with her bare eyes, she thought she could see the window without the camera, but she didn't say anything. Chloe and Grace took their turns to look through the view finder and once again saw the window with the light behind it. When Lillian looked through the viewfinder, shockingly she saw a young girl glaring back at her. Startled, she jumped back and almost fell.

"What's up?" asked Grace.

"Nothing," Lillian said. "I was just surprised to see the window again."

Lillian wasn't sure why she didn't feel comfortable enough to tell the others yet. She still dealt with issues of feeling weird compared to other kids and was still afraid of not being accepted, even though she didn't get picked on like she used to.

Lillian decided she would talk to her Kokum and Auntie about it when they had a video call.

"After lunch let's go back to the barn and figure this out," suggested Grace. Lillian shuddered, but nodded her head with Chloe in agreement.

After lunch they helped clean up and headed out the door with instructions to stay on the property and to be home at suppertime. They put on their scruffiest jeans, sweatshirts, and mud-boots so they could dig through the barn without worrying about wrecking any clothes and facing a stern look from Bernie about it.

"Looking good, girls. Good initiative; putting on your play clothes. Here, take some gummy bears with you."

They looked at each other, giggling quietly.

"Thanks!"they said, and with that they barreled out the door and straight to the barn.

"This is such a big barn," Lillian said in awe. "You could fit, like, a bunch of houses in here and still have room to keep animals. How come there are no animals except chickens?"

"My dad doesn't want to keep any animals he would have to kill," Chloe explained. "My mom's the same. I know it's weird 'cause we eat meat, but Dad said knowing something personally makes it immoral to eat. They want to be vegetarian but can't seem to commit to it. I'm okay with no other animals, unless they're gonna be pets. Dad said maybe we'll get a horse. Or a donkey and goats and maybe a pig some day. He follows a pig called Esther the Wonder Pig on Facebook. They heard this story about how some people got a pet pig because they thought it would be small forever, only for it to get huge. It happens a lot. Most people don't know how to look after pigs. Mom and Dad say that pigs are some of the smartest animals. That's a big reason why he's trying to go vegetarian." Chloe continued "He and my mom love pigs. Anyway, enough about my weird parents. Let's figure out this barn mystery."

Grace and Chloe walked slowly through the barn followed closely by Lillian.

"Everyone walk slowly and quietly, and don't talk," cautioned Chloe. All three girls peeled their eyes around the barn and listened carefully as they softly crunched through the dirt and straw on the barn floor. Grace took the camera out of her knapsack and looked through the viewfinder as they stumbled along. She didn't notice anything any different and just managed to keep herself from doing a face plant before she caught her balance again. The other two giggled and suggested she put the camera away before they repeated last year's mistake and ended up with someone breaking a bone.

Just like that morning, other than a lot of clucking chickens, nothing happened. "Let's go back to the middle and up in the loft," Chloe suggested. The girls did an about face and stood in a semi-circle around the bottom of the loft stairs. They all took a deep breath before they climbed up the stairs once again.

Chloe led the way followed by Grace, then Lillian, and they paused at the top of the stairs before going further in.

"Let's go over by where the window would be if we were looking from the outside," suggested Grace. All three went over by the wall and closed their eyes listening and waiting for something…anything.

"Hey, get your hands off my shoulders," yelled Lillian. "That's not funny!"

She opened her eyes and started swinging her arms to smack off whoever was trying to spook her. What she saw instead were Chloe and Grace staring at her in horror, their mouths hanging open almost to their knees. They were nowhere near Lillian, or her shoulders. Lillian sucked her breath in and whispered: "What the heck?"

As they stood there shaking, all three looked down at the floor at the same time and this time all of them noticed a fourth set of footprints in the hay just beside where Lillian was standing. Grace and Chloe ran screaming to the loft stairs and left Lillian standing, white-faced and unable to move. The two of them almost fell as they scrambled down the steps, nearly knocking each other over.

"Lillian," screamed Chloe. "Come on!" But Lillian remained frozen in place.

Grace joined Chloe screaming: "Get down here! Get down, now!"

Lillian ignored them both and started to take deep breaths in and out, calming herself down. She was never one to run away from something she didn't understand.

"Okay *Mishomis*. I'm like, really freaking out here. I need some help to understand what is going on. What's happening? I know it wasn't my imagination. We all felt the spooky thing and saw the footprints."

Suddenly the air became very calm and when Lillian looked down at the footprints they were gone. All the prickly little hairs on her arm and neck settled down. Her breathing was normal again and she didn't feel anyone near her. Holy crap! Suddenly Lillian heard Chloe and Grace at the bottom of the stairs, screaming for her to get away.

"I'm coming!" she said. "Stop screaming. You'll wake the dead and we don't want that right now." Lillian laughed nervously from the loft.

"Not funny, Lillian!" Grace replied. "Just get down here."

Lillian made it down the stairs and they all ran outside the barn and sat on the ground catching their breaths. All three were quiet for a few minutes, then they all started talking at the same time: "...what the heck...?" "...what happened...?" "...what touched you...?" ...did you hear anything...?" "...are we crazy...?" "...did that just happen...?" "...is my mom right...?" "we're high on sugar..." "...I can't breathe..." "...now what...?" "...don't tell anyone..." "...maybe we should tell someone..." "...why is this happening now...? "...nothing like this happened last year or ever before..." "...Oh My God..."

After babbling incoherently for a few minutes they once again fell into silence, contemplating what had just happened.

"Okay," said Lillian after another moment. "First of all, let's not say anything just yet. I want to talk with my Kokum and Auntie about this first. I'm not afraid of whatever is going on."

"Well I am," said Chloe.

"And me too," interjected Grace.

"Well, chill for now. Let me ask Kokum and Auntie first chance I get. I don't know what's going on but we don't need to be scared. At least, I don't think we do. Anyway, let's try to act normal before we go back to the house. You both look white." Lillian let out a snort. "Ha ha ha! You look white..." Chloe and Grace looked at her with blank expressions. "Oh, never mind."

When they got back to the house they noticed that they'd been in the barn longer than they thought. Wally and Leroy were back from the fields and Chloe realized that her mom was almost finished making supper already.

"Good grief, you three," Bernie said. "I was starting to think you wouldn't find your way home again."

They all looked at her blankly, afraid to say anything. "Oh, for heavens sake I'm just joking with you. What's wrong? You all look like you've just seen a ghost. Go wash up for supper now- Oh, and Lillian, your Auntie called. She's going to try and reach you tonight over video."

Lillian nodded and then scurried up the back stairs closely followed by Chloe and Grace. They were all quiet as they washed up for dinner. As they got ready to go back down and set the table Chloe reminded them “Remember, not a word to anyone.”

Chapter 8

Auntie and Kokum

AFTER DINNER AND CLEAN up all four kids went and sat on the porch.

"How was your day?" Lillian asked Wally.

"Great!" he replied. "It was fun helping dad. How 'bout you? Anything weird happen hanging out with those two?" he giggled. Grace and Chloe glared at Lillian to make sure she didn't say anything to Wally.

"Um, no not really," she said.

"Lillian," Aunt Bernie called. "Go get ready for your Kokum and Auntie to call. The rest of you stay out on the porch and give her some privacy."

Lillian ran into the house and up the back stairs and set her tablet on her lap. She stared at it and tapped her feet impatiently, willing it to ring. Finally, it did. When Lillian answered, she could see Kokum and Auntie's faces on the screen.

"*Aaniin aaniin,* my beautiful granddaughter," said Kokum.

"Hey sweetheart," Auntie chimed in. "How's it going? We miss you."

"Oh Auntie and Kokum, I miss you too, but I'm okay here. Everyone is good to me, but I need your help. I've come across a mystery and I don't know what to do!" Lillian shook her head, but remembered something important. "I'm sorry! I forgot to ask how you are, and how everyone is doing! What about the sick people, how are they?"

Auntie answered, "We are good, my girl. We are very busy going from home to home helping with our sick. It is hard with having to change gowns and masks and wash our hands between the homes, but it is good. I hope you are listening to Chloe's mom and not venturing off the farm on one of your little walkabouts."

"No, Auntie, but there is something I need help with from you both."

Kokum and Auntie looked at her expectantly. Lillian just stared back, because she wasn't sure how to start. Now that she was in the quiet of the girls' bedroom, what happened to them in the barn seemed too weird to be real. Lillian thought maybe they had let their imaginations run away on them.

"Hmm... Well..." Lillian said. "Something kinda weird is going on in the barn. I'm not sure if it's real or our imaginations. I don't know how to figure it out and I was going to ask for help, but maybe I'll wait for a few days before I tell you all of it..." Kokum and Auntie nodded in encouragement, so Lillian kept going.

"I think we might be seeing a spirit," Lillian blurted. "But I'm not a hundred percent sure, 'cause honestly that big ol' barn is pretty weird all on its own. I think I saw something, but Grace and Chloe said that even before I came they saw a window that isn't really there. They can only see it through the viewfinder on this old camera they found in the barn and that's the only way I could see it at first. But now, I can see it without the camera. I haven't even told them that yet—" Lillian finally stopped for air.

Kokomis and Auntie looked at each other with knowing expressions.

"Has this being tried to talk to you yet?" Kokum asked.

"No," replied Lillian, "but I think it wants to. I kept seeing it in the corner of my eye. I'm not afraid, but Chloe and Grace are, so I'm not letting them know what I can see. I'm not telling Chloe's parents yet either, 'cause they'll just think we're on a sugar high. I think her dad is afraid of this sort of stuff too."

"I suggest you talk to Wally," said Kokum.

"Seriously?" said Lillian. "He's just a kid. What would he know?"

Kokomis and Auntie smiled at each other again. "He may be, as you put it, 'just a kid,' Lillian," Kokum said "But talk with him about this anyway. He spends lots of time in the bush and in the barn. Never underestimate the power of a child. Remember, you are also a child."

Lillian hummed and reflected on her Kokum's words. "Okay," Lillian said. "I guess you're right. Let me check this out and I'll report to you in a few days." Lillian gazed at Blue Bear to see if he had something to offer but he just sat there in his quiet thoughtful way.

"Auntie, Kokum, can you talk to Chloe's dad? He seems really sad sometimes. I know it has something to do with our culture and his family but he won't talk to his family here." Auntie and Kokum nodded and Lillian smiled. Lillian glanced at her hands trying to figure out what to say next. She was thinking about how lucky she was now that she had discovered her Indigenous culture and wanted Chloe's dad to be happier too.

She couldn't quite figure out everything that was going on around her so she just sighed instead. That was much easier than thinking too hard. "I guess I should go now," Lillian said. "Love you. I hope everyone there gets better soon. I promise we are staying on the property and not going anywhere."

"We love you too," said both Auntie and Kokomis.

Lillian disconnected the call and put her tablet down on the bed. She sat for a minute thinking about what Auntie and Kokum had just said. They didn't seem to think anything she had shared with them was weird. What struck Lillian as odd was that they wanted her to talk to little kid Wally.

"Huh," she muttered to herself. "I'll have to figure that one out without telling the girls."

With that thought in mind, she raced downstairs again and went back out on the porch with the other kids. They all looked up at her expectantly.

"Uh...Kokum and Auntie send their love to everyone," Lillian said. "They are very busy with all the sick people but they're staying safe and being careful, and that's about it." She looked at Wally but decided now was not the time to mention what her Auntie and Kokum had suggested.

Wally and Bertram wandered off into the fields for some last minute freedom before it was time for bed. The three girls huddled head to head on the porch, whispering to one another and conspiring a plan for the barn. "'K, spit out the truth, Lillian," said Grace. "What did they say to do about the light in the window?"

"And don't lie..." added Chloe.

"Well," started Lillian. "They both said we should try to find out more before we decide what to do, and just for the record, neither of them think we're crazy or hallucinating or imagining things. They didn't actually use those words, but I know that's what they meant."

Grace and Chloe bobbed their heads up and down, agreeing with Lillian that indeed they were not imagining things. "Okay," Grace said. "I say we go full out investigative mode tomorrow. We can spend the day in the barn and maybe question your mom and dad about some history surrounding this place. Sound good?"

Chloe and Lillian looked at one another, shrugged their shoulders and said, "Yep, sounds good."

"Girls, Wally, it's time to come in," Aunt Bernie called through the door. "Oh, good grief. Where's Wally now?"

"Don't worry mom, we'll go get him," Chloe offered. The three girls jumped off the porch and went running in the direction of the pond. They knew where to find him.

"Wally! Bertram! Come on home now!' They all took turns yelling for them.

"*Wewiibitaan,* Wally!" shouted Lillian. Grace and Chloe stared at her. "What?" said Lillian. "Sometimes Wally responds better to Anishinaabek language. I don't know very many words but I use the few I know when I can. *Wewiibitaan* just means hurry up. Chloe, you should try to use some words every once in a while."

"Whatever," responded Chloe, but they did see Wally and Bertram running towards them. When he got to them, he said "*Aaniin*" and looked shyly at Lillian. Lillian grinned "Hi, back atcha. Good use of your words, Wally. That's how we learn."

They walked slowly back to the house, not really wanting to go in. Had they taken the time to look back at the barn they might have noticed the flashing light coming from the big barn window that did not exist.

Chapter 9

Up the Loft Stairs

THE NEXT MORNING Lillian tried to find a way to talk with Wally by himself, but the opportunity didn't happen. Wally had such a blast with his dad the day before that he asked to go with him again, and much to Wally's surprise and happiness Leroy said yes. Aunt Bernie told the girls she had a lot of little things to do that day around the farm and that they would have to keep themselves entertained. She had put some sandwiches and drinks in the fridge in case she wasn't there for lunch, and the girls would be able to call her cell phone if they needed her.

Bernie was going to be all over the farm that day, checking things out and visiting with Leroy and Wally. She also had a video meeting to attend. The girls told her they'd be fine as they also had plans and knew how to get to her quickly if they needed her.

Bernie snapped her head up when she heard that the girls 'had plans'.

"What plans?" she asked suspiciously. "I hope you three aren't planning any crazy ideas in your head."

"Um… No, Mom, of course not," Chloe muttered. "We're just gonna hang around the house and barn."

The girls headed out the door and made a beeline straight to the barn before Bernie could ask any more questions.

"Holy," said Chloe. "You'd think we were going to do something stupid like rob a bank, the way she was looking at us."

Lillian and Grace grinned at each other.

"Well she's not far off," said Lillian.

"Except for the bank-robbing part," said Grace. "That's the one thing we know we won't do today."

They chuckled as they got closer to the barn.

"Race ya!" yelled Chloe.

With that challenge, all three ran as fast as they could, whipping through the tall grass and weeds that surrounded the barn. They threw themselves down as they got to the doors and gasped for breath.

"Wow, you're fast," Grace managed to wheeze to Lillian. "I can barely breathe right now." Lillian grinned shyly.

"Okay," interrupted Chloe. "Let's get to business and figure out what's going on in this barn. I say we stick close together and don't wander off on our own. I know something or someone is up there. Get the camera out and let's see what happens. Who's got it?"

Grace held the camera up. They all looked at where it sat in her hand and then they all looked up at where the window wasn't. Since Grace was holding the camera she looked through it first.

"I don't believe it," she said. "It's there again. It has a really bright light coming out of it now."

Grace lowered the camera and looked at the barn with just her eyes, and still there were no signs of a window or reflections of any sort.

"You look, Lillian."

"No, let Chloe look first."

Lillian didn't want to tell them that she could see the window perfectly without the camera now. She could see the bright light too, but after a moment she thought that she could also see a shape inside that light. Lillian gave her head a shake and looked again, and this time she was absolutely sure that there was some sort of human figure inside the light.

"Yep, I see it too," said Chloe. "The window and the light. I guess we're not on a sugar high. Your turn Lillian."

Lillian held the camera to her eyes for show.

"Yep, I see it too," she said before she quickly put the camera away. They all stared at each other, not sure what to do.

"Well," said Chloe. "It's time for a plan. What do we do?"

"I say we go inside the barn and see if we can spot anything in there," Grace suggested. They all nodded and went just beyond the doors. Nothing seemed to happen when they did that.

"Okay, now what?" asked Chloe.

"How about we go into the loft and see what we can see?" suggested Lillian.

"Oh, I dunno if that's a good idea," Chloe moaned. "I'm not allowed up there ever. It was bad enough when we went up there last time."

"Fine, I'll go up myself," was Lillian's response.

"No!" Chloe and Grace yelled.

"Remember, we stay together no matter what," said Grace.

"I don't care," Lillian said. "I'm going up. You

can wait at the bottom of the stairs or come up with me. It's your choice."

Chloe and Grace looked at each other and shrugged their shoulders.

"Fine," said Chloe. "We'll come up with you. But we stick together up there. If anyone finds out, we'll be grounded from this barn for the rest of the summer. I guarantee you that."

Together, one behind the other, Lillian led them up the loft stairs.

Chapter 10

All By Themselves

LILLIAN CAUTIOUSLY PEERED across the floor of the loft through all the bundles of straw and hay. The loft seemed bigger than the last time they were up there. She crawled up and sat waiting for the other two to get up the stairs. While Lillian sat in anticipation of what she might see, the others started to shake a little from fright, knowing they were all by themselves at the farm, without any adults.

"I don't like it up here," said Grace.

"Me neither," said Chloe.

"It's fine," Lillian muttered, more to herself than the others. "There's nothing here," she said, not really convinced.

They all sat quietly with their eyes darting around the loft — waiting, not really sure what they were waiting for. After a few minutes, absolutely nothing happened. They decided to walk around to see if they could make something occur but still nothing. They looked through the camera's viewfinder but all they saw was what they could see with their eyes. Finally, they decided to go back down and see what the chickens were up to in their section of the barn. Eventually they got bored and went out and ran around in the bush instead, trying to scare one another.

"Well this sucks for summer adventures," Chloe said. "Let's go back to the house and eat lunch." Chloe sent a quick text to her mom with a heart emoji and told her that they were on their way home before they trudged back to the house, disappointed in their non-adventure.

By the time they arrived, Chloe's mom had returned the text. It said that Wally would be hanging out with them for the next couple of weeks because Leroy was going to be working with dangerous farm machinery in the field and didn't want Wally in harm's way. Chloe groaned and read the text out to the others. They all groaned a bit but knew not to protest too loudly. It wasn't that they didn't want Wally around, but he would definitely hinder Chloe and Grace's adventure plans… or so they thought.

Lillian was happy because it would give her a chance to talk to Wally. After they ate, another text came in from Bernie instructing the girls to stay out of trouble, to be home for suppertime and, of course, to make sure someone had a phone with them. Life was good. They were happy.

Chapter 11

Taking Time With Wally

THE NEXT WEEK was uneventful. Each morning the girls would go to the barn, usually with Wally and Bertram in tow. Sometimes Wally stayed with his mom and the girls went adventuring alone. They had yet to see anything up in the loft but they still saw the window with the light when they looked through the camera viewfinder. Lillian continued to see it without, but still didn't tell the others.

One day Lillian asked Wally if he wanted to go for a walk in the woods and practice some of his language. Earlier, Chloe and Grace had replied "no thanks" to the same offer, so Lillian knew she could finally talk with Wally. Every night when Auntie and Kokum called, they asked Lillian if she had spoken with Wally yet. She kept having to say that she hadn't had the chance to talk to him without Chloe and Grace around. During their last conversation Auntie and Kokum told Lillian to make the time. So here she was, doing just that.

"Hey, Wally," Lillian started. "Do you talk to anything or anyone out here when you're alone?"

"Of course I do," Wally said, very matter-of-fact about it. "All the spirits of everything are here for us to talk to."

Lillian looked at him in amazement.

"Really?"

"Of course," he replied. "You know that, Lillian. Just because my family doesn't believe doesn't mean that I don't. I know spirits are there because they talk to me. I just don't let my family know because they just think I'm nuts and I'll outgrow my fantasy world."

Wally bent down to pick up a small rock that was glimmering in the sunlight. He rolled it around carefully in his hands.

"That's okay with me," he added. "I don't need them involved. They're the ones who miss out. They ignore me most of the time because I'm still a kid, and that's okay too." After rolling the rock around a little longer, he put it in his pocket.

"I know you've been wanting to talk to me, Lillian. I could feel it."

"Wow," Lillian said. "You are amazing." Lillian had a hard time finding the words she needed to start the conversation about the spirit in the barn and was looking around her head for them.

"Just spit it out," Wally said. "You want to talk to me about your experiences in the barn."

"Whoa....What the heck, Wally. How did you know?" Lillian was in shock as she listened to Wally.

"Hey," he said. "I don't say much, but that doesn't mean I'm stupid or I don't know what's going on around me. Sometimes you learn more by being quiet, as you know."

Wally looked at Lillian with a shy smile. "Anyway, let's you and me go to the barn. I think someone wants to meet you."

Lillian was in such a shocked state at everything Wally was saying that she just followed him without question to the barn.

"Holy, Wally!" she said. "You kinda freak me out a little, but in a good way. My Kokum said to talk with you and I'm glad she did. You're pretty cool."

The two of them went into the barn and stood quietly for a few minutes. Bertram sat and looked straight up the loft stairs with his ears forward and his hackles raised. He made a low guttural sound that was almost a growl but not quite. After a moment Lillian looked at Wally and said, "Well, let's see what happens," and walked up the stairs.

Chapter 12

A Hand on Lillian's Shoulder

LILLIAN FELT IT as soon as they entered the loft. It wasn't a particular feeling she could describe but one that felt other-worldly in her mind. She felt like she was floating just above the straw and hay, but when she looked at her feet they were firmly planted on the floor.

Wally gave her a strange look and said, "If you're not afraid, Lillian, me and Bertram are gonna wait for you outside the barn. I don't know what's up here or why, but I don't think I'm supposed to be here."

Several muddled up thoughts popped into Lillian's mind but the one that shone through was, *Wow... Wally's one cool little dude.*

"I'm fine," she said. "I'm not afraid, Wally. I'll be okay, but I'll yell or scream if I need you." With those words Wally and Bertram scurried down the stairs and out of the barn. Lillian was alone, or was she?

Lillian crept across the loft floor toward the window, that wasn't there.

"Okay," she whispered. "I'm here alone. Come out, come out whatever you are, but don't try to scare me, 'cause I'm not afraid." Lillian's words were hesitant as her lips trembled in fear. When something finally happened, she felt it more than she saw it. It felt like something or someone was staring at Lillian, and she thought she could feel a breath on her neck.

"That's enough!" she yelled out bravely. "You can't hurt me. I know that, so quit acting like you're bigger than me…and tougher, and…braver…and scarier, and...and I don't know! I don't know what you are or who you are or what you want, but stop playing around. We left you alone for over a week, so figure out how to talk to me, if you are a thing that can talk." Lillian darted her eyes around. Once again, she kept catching a glimpse of something fluttering just outside her field of vision. "Hey, you…thing, I'm talking to you."

Lillian was talking way braver than she felt but that was how she talked whenever she got bullied at school, or when she was afraid in a new situation.

"Okay. I'm gonna sit down here and wait for you to do something."

Lillian sat on a bale of hay and waited. "Hey, thing. This ain't no movie. There's no music that'll tell you when to appear. Just do it."

At first, nothing more happened, but then she felt it. It was like a whoosh sound and a very gentle breeze across her neck and face. Lillian spun her head around and still all she could see was a glimpse of something. The straw and hay started to spin very gently and slowly around her.

"What the holy crap?" Lillian closed her eyes unable to see through the dust that had started to pick up. She felt a hand on her shoulder. She wanted to faint but tried to remain calm.

Suddenly the straw and hay stopped spinning and the hand on her shoulder was gone! Lillian wasn't sure if she imagined it or if she actually heard a very faint whisper saying "soon."

She opened her eyes, expecting to find Wally behind her, but he wasn't there. Then, just as quickly as everything had gone weird, everything felt normal again.

Lillian was a little shaken up but pulled herself together. After looking around the loft one more time she went down and out of the barn to look for Wally. She didn't have to look very hard, because both he and Bertram were sitting just outside, waiting for her.

"We were waiting in case you needed us," he stated. "I heard you yelling and talking. Are you okay?"

"Yeah," Lillian replied. "I just gotta figure out what happened, and why. Let's go back to the house."

The two of them were lost in their own thoughts, but as they walked back, Bertram continued to cast the occasional glance over his shoulder and emit that low growl at the barn.

Chapter 13

Dashes and Dots

WHEN THEY GOT BACK Wally wandered off with Bertram over to the big catulpa tree while Lillian went inside to find where Chloe and Grace were. Bernie was working in the kitchen. She told Lillian that Chloe and Grace were up in their room working on some sort of project.

As soon as Lillian ran up the stairs they were all over her.

"Holy, you were gone a long time," Chloe said. "How much language did you speak with Wally?"

"Huh?" Lillian answered. "What language?"

"Are you okay?" Grace asked.

"Yeah, you look stunned," added Chloe. "You went to practice some language with Wally, remember? Duh!"

"Oh, yeah...No, we didn't do language. He

ran off with Bertram and I went into the barn."

"What?" they both yelled. They glared at her giving her the stink eye. "You went without us?"

"What the heck?"

"What happened?"

"Well, I'm not sure, but I think it tried to speak to me. I still can't see what it is, but I swear I heard it say something. I dunno, I think I felt a hand, and now that I'm a little calmer, I think it was a kid's hand, or.... Who knows? Maybe it's a space alien that speaks English. Quick, look through the camera and see."

Chloe grabbed the camera and looked through. "Holy moly," she said. "It looks like a real window now, and I think I see someone. It might be an alien. You look, Grace."

Grace reluctantly took the camera and hesitated before looking through. She went pale and whispered. "No, no, no! It can't be. I see it too. I think it is an alien."

Grace dropped the camera, and all three girls just sat, staring at each other, then staring out the window at the barn. "What? seriously?" Chloe said "We have an alien in the barn? An alien ghost?"

Lillian looked at the barn. Now she could see

everything without looking through the camera and that included seeing a small, bright, 'alien' in the window. The light was getting brighter all the time and seemed to fade in and out, almost like a flashing light. *Wait a minute*, she thought to herself. *Is that Morse code?* "Nah, that's just crazy," she mumbled aloud.

"What's crazy?" asked Grace.

"Uh, nothing," Lillian replied. "I was just thinking out loud. Hey, do either of you two know Morse code?"

"No," Chloe said. "But my dad has a book on it. I'll go check the office. Why?"

"Well, maybe I've been hanging out in the barn too much, but I'm wondering if the light we can see dimming and brightening all the time is Morse code. Just a thought."

"Okay, I'll go look."

Chloe ran down the stairs and returned a few minutes later with a book.

"Here it is, I knew dad had a book on it." Chloe shuffled through the pages. "Look, here's a page that shows the alphabet with the dots and dashes beside each letter."

"Wow," exclaimed Grace. "Your dad has just about everything"

"I don't know if this is even what's happening," Lillian piped in. "But tonight after we've gone to bed let's pay attention to the shining brightness. This is like that show *Stranger Things* when that one kid tries to communicate with his mom through the flashing Christmas lights. Maybe this is what this alien ghost is trying to do to communicate with us."

After supper that night the girls claimed tiredness and went up to bed at the same time as Wally. Bernie thought it a little weird, but didn't give it too much thought. They had been outside most of the day after all, so they could be tired.

Chloe opened up to the page with the chart of all the dots and dashes, and all three sat and stared at the barn waiting for something, but they weren't sure what. Chloe and Grace took turns looking through the camera, while Lillian just stared at the window that wasn't there. Suddenly, it happened. The light started fading in and out in what seemed like no particular pattern. They went to pass the camera to Lillian but she shook her head.

"I gotta 'fess up guys. I can see it without looking through the camera." The two girls dropped their jaws to their chins in amazement and shock. "You what?" they cried.

"Sorry. I didn't want to tell you sooner. I was afraid I would scare you." Chloe and Grace still wore shocked faces. "And I see I was right."

"How is that even possible?" Grace wanted to know.

"Why can't we do that too?" Chloe added. Lillian shrugged.

"I don't know, but let's not worry about that now. Let's try to figure out if there is a pattern to the lights. I noticed that when it goes dim it only stays dim for a second or so but when it goes brighter it stays bright a little bit longer. Let's say dim is a dot and bright is a dash and see how that works."

All three got a piece of paper and pencil and stared at the light. "Okay, one of you look through the camera and the other one can put the dashes and dots onto the paper. I'll do the same and we'll see what we end up with."

--- -.-- .-.. . .-. .-.

--- -.-- .-.. . .-. --- -.--

--- -.-- .-.. . .-. .-.

--- -.-- .-.. . .-. --- -.--

--- -.-- .-.. . .-. .-.

--- -.-- .-.. . .-.

By the time the pattern started over for the third time, their pages were covered in dashes and dots. It didn't look like a message yet, but together they peered at the Morse code book.

"Okay, lets see what we have," Lillian said. "O-Y-L.... Not making sense yet... the next letters, you guys? E-R-O-Y...That still doesn't make sense. 'Oyl Eroy.'"

"What does that even mean?" asked Grace. "Oyl Eroy."

They copied as best they could the dots and dashes and they kept getting OYL EROY over and over.

"I don't get it," muttered Lillian. "It doesn't make sense."

"Lights out, girls!" Bernie called. "I'll be up in a minute to say goodnight."

Grace quickly stuffed the camera and papers under the mattress, and Chloe checked to make sure there was nothing else suspicious in their room. The three of them then jumped into their beds with one last sideways glance at the barn in search of the alien ghost.

As they drifted off to sleep Lillian wondered how an alien would know Morse code and English. Maybe it was trying to speak in alien. She fell asleep with Oyl Eroy tumbling around in her head.

Suddenly, in the middle of the night Lillian bolted up awake and yelled out, “Leroy! It’s trying to say Leroy!” and promptly fell asleep again.

Chapter 14

More and More Curious

THE NEXT MORNING as the household was waking up, Grace remembered hearing someone yell out in the middle of the night.

"Hey, did either of you wake up last night? I heard something, but I couldn't figure out who it was or what they were yelling."

"No," Chloe and Lillian replied in unison.

"That's weird," Grace mused. "Oh well."

After breakfast, Wally asked his dad if he could spend the day with him and to his delight, Leroy said yes. That meant the girls could spend the day in the barn and not have to worry about Wally. Strict instructions came from Bernie about what was off-limits and when to come in for lunch. Grace, Chloe, and Lillian left with a knapsack full of water and snacks and the camera. The grass was getting pretty high in the fields around the barn so they played at scrunching down in it and trying to scare each other. As they got closer to the barn, they all seemed to automatically tense up and they drew closer together, linking arms with one another as if for protection. It actually made them feel braver.

After all the goofing around before getting to the barn, they finally arrived. Still arm in arm, they stopped at the big barn door entry and just stared at it. "Okay, this is it," Grace declared. "I feel it! Today we are going to solve this mystery. Hopefully the alien or whatever it is will come out and show itself."

"Hope it speaks English," Chloe chimed in.

"I hope we find out what it is, why it is, and what it wants," added Lillian.

And with that, all three crossed the doorway into the barn.

"Something's different in here today but I don't know what it is," whispered Lillian.

Grace nodded, saying,"I feel it too."

"Me three," added Chloe.

"Okay, deep breaths. Let's do this."

Being the bravest of the three, Lillian led the way up the loft stairs closely followed by Chloe and then Grace.

"Something's not right," Chloe said. "It's too quiet. Even the chickens aren't clucking."

Chloe wasn't used to not hearing them. Her skin started to prickle up like it always did when she was afraid. Grace felt super cold all of a sudden and Lillian, well, Lillian just got more curious.

"I dunno," Chloe muffled into Lillian's back. "This still doesn't feel right. We're not supposed to be up here... This doesn't feel right." Lillian responded with a "Shhh..."

Slowly, slowly, slowly they crept forward arms linked together once again for added bravery, and then it happened. The straw and hay all started swirling around the three of them, making an eerie whistling noise that got higher and higher in pitch. It started to move the girls off their feet and they desperately kept their arms linked, trying to stay steady.

As suddenly as the floating started, it stopped and the three girls found themselves heaped in a pile in the middle of the loft. They screamed, and screamed, and screamed some more, until Lillian composed herself and yelled, "Enough! Screaming isn't going to help. I don't know what just happened, but we are fine. So stop." With that, they all stopped and sat silently but that didn't help the situation. The hay and straw was still moving around but not like before. It was kind of like someone was kicking it with their feet or throwing handfuls of it around the loft. Then, magically, everything came to a halt.

Chapter 15

Remembering the Message

After sitting quietly for a few minutes, the girls got up, brushed themselves off, and looked around the loft. No one even bothered with the camera at that point. Lillian felt the room fade away and thought she was going to faint. She could hear her name being yelled over and over, "Lillian…!" "Lillian…!" "What's happening to you…?" "You're disappearing…!" "Quick, grab our hands…!" "Hurry up…!" "You're turning to dust or something, hurry up…!" and then she remembered the message she received when she had woken up in the middle of the night.

"Leroy!" Lillian cried. "Holy crap. The alien thing was trying to spell 'Leroy!'" and with that, she passed out.

Meanwhile, Chloe and Grace were once again screaming as they saw their friend fade before their eyes. “Come back, Lillian! Come back!” they yelled and each grabbed Lillian’s hands, trying to keep her from disappearing. As she was fading they heard her yell “Leroy!” and as soon as that happened she started to reappear. As they pulled her, she fell into them and passed out.

“Holy crap…” “What the heck…What just happened…?” said Grace.

“I better go get my mom,” Chloe yelled, struggling to her feet and down the steps so she could run to the house.

“Okay,” Grace muttered. “Okay. Oh, Lillian, what just happened? Where are you? What have we done? I knew this was a bad idea.” Grace felt Lillian squeezing her hand.

“No,” she rasped. “No, don’t get anyone yet! I’m fine. I’m fine, honestly, I’m fine. I think this thing was just trying to get our attention. I’m not hurt, look.”

Lillian stood up and moved her arms and legs around to show she wasn’t hurt.

“Chloe!” Lillian yelled out to her. “Chloe, it was spelling your dad’s name. We just got the dashes dots and spaces all mixed up. As soon as I yelled ‘Leroy’ it stopped doing weird things.

Things got very strange in the barn.

It wanted us to understand. I don't think it's an alien, I think it's human."

With that, Lillian sat back down and said: "Now we gotta figure out what your dad has to do with this. Let's just think about it and try to ask your mom some questions at lunch time that might help us." Chloe checked her phone to see what time it was, "Holy moly you guys, we gotta run. It's past when we were supposed to go in for lunch. Can you run okay, Lillian?"

"Yeah, I'm fine." Chloe quickly texted her mom with 'be there in a sec' and all three bounded down the stairs. In their haste they left Grace's backpack behind with everything in it, except for the camera which Chloe was carrying. What they didn't see was the backpack floating in the air as they ran in fear from the barn.

"Mom, we're here for lunch!" Chloe yelled as she ran in the door.

"It's about time. Where have you three been? You're an hour late!" scolded back her mom.

"Um… well, uh, actually..." Chloe stumbled on her words so Grace burst in.

“What she’s trying to say is we lost track of time ’cause we were playing out behind the barn in the bush by the pond.” Lillian just pondered the situation quietly.

“Never mind,” Bernie said. “Just don’t do it again. I was worried something might have happened to you.” With that statement all three girls looked at each other. Bernie narrowed her eyes. “You all look very guilty about something. What’s going on? What are you three up to?”

“Nothing mom, honest!” Chloe insisted. “But uh…. We were just wondering… Did anything unusual ever happen at this farm before we moved here? Y’know, like aliens landing here or something like that…” Chloe gave a nervous laugh, and Bernie looked at her daughter long and hard.

“How many of those gummy bears did you take with you to the barn today?” she said. “That’s it for candy. You’re all cut off for the next few days.”

“Not that many, Mom, honest! We forgot we even had them! Here, I’ll show you — Oh, shoot, we left our backpack in the barn.”

“We’ll get it and prove it!” Grace said. “Please, don’t cut us off….”

"Hmm," Bernie said, arms crossed. "We'll see after lunch."

As they sat and ate lunch together Chloe tried to get info from her mom again.

"Did something happen to dad here?" she asked.

Bernie snapped her head up and stared at her daughter.

"Why would you ask that?"

Chloe stumbled with something to say.

"Well.... Just because he's so grumpy sometimes. He never wants to talk about anything to do with family... and he seems to be angry with Kokum. I thought... maybe something had happened here."

"Nothing ever happened here," Bernie said. "Your dad has his own demons to battle, just like we all do. It's not my story to tell. We need to be respectful. He'll tell you when he feels the time is right." And with that, Bernie started mumbling about all the chores she had to do, and they completely avoided the topic of Uncle Leroy.

Lunch was pretty quiet after that, with everyone lost in their own thoughts. As they were cleaning up and getting ready to head to the barn, Bernie told Lillian that her Kokum was going to be calling that night and to be ready for it. Apparently she had something important to share with her.

"Okay," Lillian responded. "Thank you"

It seemed particularly hot outside as they walked through the tall grass. Everything was still. There was no rustling of leaves or birdsong and even the grass seemed browner than before lunch. All of them felt a little off kilter as they trudged to the barn yet again.

Chapter 16

The Fog Gets Thicker

WHEN THEY PASSED THROUGH the barn doors, they *felt* the difference before they really *saw* or *heard* it. Something was different, but they couldn't figure it out — well not at first. Slowly, they climbed the loft stairs. Then, as they looked around they saw it. They started shaking and grabbed each other for support.

"Holy crap," were the first words out of Grace's mouth.

"I think I'm gonna puke," added Chloe.

"Holy moly," said Lillian.

"Nope. Nuh-uh. This is definitely not our imaginations."

There, spelled out on the loft floor with straw was a single word: LEROY. Hanging up in the rafters, way up above their heads, was the forgotten knapsack. They wouldn't be able to get it down without a ladder.

"Okay, now I'm telling my mom," Chloe whispered.

"Yep, it's time," agreed Grace. To their surprise Lillian said: "No! Not yet. Let me talk to my Kokum and Auntie tonight. Then we'll decide."

"Lillian you're nuts," Chloe hissed. "This is way too much for us now! What if some lunatic is coming in here when we're not around and doing this to scare us? That's only thing that actually makes sense, and if that's what's going on my mom and dad need to know!"

They all started shaking uncontrollably in fear. "No!" Lillian yelled this time. "All that other stuff that happened was not because of some crazy stranger. You both know that. Just give me till tomorrow and then we'll tell your parents. I promise. Please, trust me. I know this has something to do with your dad. I just don't know how yet."

They argued it back and forth for a few minutes then all of them finally agreed one more day but that was all. They came up with equal reasons as to telling or not telling but for some reason none of them understood, they all agreed — one more day.

No one was in the mood to do anything more, so they went back to the house. Bernie was surprised when all three showed up looking so glum and unhappy.

"What's the matter?" she asked them. "You all look like you just had a fight or something."

"No, Mom. We're all good, honest. We're just tired from running around too much. We're gonna go lie down for a while."

"Where's that knapsack you were going to show me?" Chloe shared a look with the other girls and hesitated.

"Oh, darn it," Lillian piped up. "We left it in the barn again."

"How convenient," Bernie said. "Guess you can't show me those gummy bears then. No more candy for three days, and no argument."

The girls all shuffled upstairs, still trying not to freak out too much about what they'd seen in the barn. They climbed onto their beds each wrapped in their own thoughts about the barn.

Lillian hugged her blue bear and tried to make more sense out of the word 'Leroy,' but the more she thought about it the more tired she became, and she soon fell asleep. Chloe and Grace soon joined Lillian in sleep as well.

"Lillian," someone said. "Lillian, listen to me. I don't have much time left." Lillian shook her head back and forth trying to clear the mist from her eyes until she realized she was actually encased in fog. "What the heck?" she said. "Hey, what's going on? Where's all this fog coming from? Where am I?"

"Focus, Lillian!" said the voice. "Listen to me. You're my only hope. Believe in yourself. You don't need to know or understand everything, Just believe that this is possible, that you can hear and understand me. Listen to your Kokum. *Wabi! Nondam!* See and hear.... I can't stay..." The voice, wherever it came from, was starting to fade.

"Hey, hey, hey!" yelled Lillian. "Who are you? Where are you? What are you?!"

She tried harder to clear her eyes and see, but the fog just got thicker.

"Lillian, Lillian, hey Lillian, wake up!" shouted Grace and Chloe as they shook her feet. "Wake up! You're having a nightmare, wake up!"

Lillian bolted straight up into a sitting position. "What just happened? Where did all that fog go? Did you hear it? Did you see it?"

"No offense," said Chloe. "But I think you're losing it. There's no fog, we're in our bedroom."

"Man, maybe Aunt Bernie is right in cutting us off the candy," said Grace.

Lillian looked at them.

"No," she stated. "Something's going on and it has nothing to do with candy. I need to speak to my Kokum and Auntie as soon as possible. Hold on, one of you look through the camera and tell me what you see."

Chloe got the camera first and looked through it. "I can still see the window, but now I'm seeing that alien ghost... floating or maybe it's like...waving or something. It's all foggy and blurry, though. I can't even see that bright light now."

Grace took her turn with the camera and looked. "Same here. This just gets weirder all the time. Are there even such things as aliens? There'd have to be for there to be ghost aliens, right?" Chloe just shrugged.

"All I know is that it's creeping me out now more than when it was just the window."

Chapter 17

Sacred Medicines

LILLIAN FELT BETTER, well sorta better, about things after Chloe and Grace looked through the camera and saw exactly what she saw with her own eyes. They decided to stop looking and go downstairs to do something else. Bernie found them huddled together in the living room, whispering to each other.

"I don't know what you girls are up to, but I have a feeling it's probably something you shouldn't be doing. I certainly hope you aren't going up into the loft in the barn. You know that's not safe."

The girls just looked up at Bernie and smiled because none of them wanted to be the one to lie about what they were doing. It didn't fool Bernie, but she didn't push it.

"Grace, I could use some help with supper because Wally and your Uncle Leroy will be home soon. Chloe you too. Lillian, your Auntie is going to call you in about ten minutes, so find somewhere you feel comfortable to talk with her. She said it's very important."

Lillian decided to go wait in her room for the video call. It didn't take long.

"*Kwe kwe,* my girl," Auntie said. "How are you? How goes your quest? Your Kokum wants to talk with you."

Kokum's face came on the screen. "*Kwe kwe,* sweet girl. We love and miss you. We don't have a lot of time. Tell me, what is going on with the spirit in the barn?"

Lillian told Kokum everything that had happened including the dream she had just had.

"Kokum, I thought it might be an alien ghost but it spoke to me in English in my dream." Kokum paused for a minute before answering.

"Lillian, I'm going to tell you some things that will help you understand better what is going on, and your role in all of it. I have been talking with Chloe's father, Leroy, and his mother, who is Chloe's Kokum. We have found the source of his sadness, but that is his story. It is not for me to tell. Tonight, Lillian, be ready with your sacred medicines and put them down, and you smudge, and you pray. Tomorrow you must also put tobacco down at the barn and you will get your answers. You must believe and have faith. You will need all your friends with you, including Wally. This spirit wants to talk to you and you have not been open. Open your heart to it.... We must go. We will be done our work here soon. The sick are getting better and the healthy are staying healthy. We will see you soon. Tomorrow you will talk with Chloe's mom and dad after your work in the barn. You will understand tomorrow. *Kisagin*, I love you."

"I love you too, Kokum and Auntie."

After the call was over, Lillian sat alone, thinking of what her Kokum had said to her. Lillian couldn't understand all of it, but Kokum said she would understand the next day and Lillian believed her Kokum. She would listen, and be open, and believe. Lillian now understood that this spirit was not about her. She also knew now that there wasn't really an alien in the barn, but, to be honest, she was a little disappointed to find that out.

Wally and Leroy returned to the house while Lillian was upstairs, and as she scurried down to greet them, she remembered what Kokomis said about Wally. "*Kwe*, Wally," she said to him. "Good to see you."

"*Kwe,* Lillian."

"Hey, Wally, I need your help today and tomorrow. Please, and *miigwech*."

"Anything," he said. Lillian smiled.

"Gather the medicines you have and meet me out at the pond."

"On it."

The two of them met up out at the pond a few minutes later. Wally showed her the medicines and showed her his abalone shell and they lay them down in a display, as Kokum had instructed.

"Okay," Lillian said. "Let's smudge and pray. We're gonna need a lot of help tomorrow."

Wally grabbed the big wooden matches that he had brought with him. They had some white sage, tobacco, cedar, and sweetgrass, the four sacred medicines which they lit up and let smoulder in the abalone shell. They then held their hands over the fire and guided the smoke over their eyes, nose, mouth, ears, and heart.

Lillian and Wally meet at the pond to smudge with sacred medicines.

"Don't worry if we don't do it exactly right," Lillian said. "My Kokum says that's highly overrated. She says that if we do it from the heart and with good intentions then that is the right way. It's between us and the Creator, not us and other humans."

Wally smiled at Lillian's words because he was always being told that the way he did things was wrong by those who were more 'traditional.'

They prayed together in silence, not realizing that the rest of the family were watching them from the house. They prayed with Wally and Lillian in their own way, although they weren't really sure why.

That evening as everyone was getting ready for bed Lillian reminded Wally she would need his help the next day.

"Tomorrow is a big day," she said to Wally and the girls. "Tomorrow I believe our mystery will be solved. I truly believe it." Grace and Chloe looked at Lillian, puzzled, but after all they had witnessed in the barn, they didn't question her.

Chapter 18

Not a Day for Bertram

IT WAS A BEAUTIFUL MORNING when everyone woke up. The sun was shining and there was a light breeze, just enough to keep it cool and blow the mosquitoes away. It was the kind of day that put a smile on everyone's face, even grumpy Leroy. The kids and Bertram all went downstairs at the same time encouraged by the smell of eggs and toast. Bernie looked up at them as they trudged into the kitchen. "French toast with maple syrup from the farm for today's menu," she said.

"What's going on?" asked Chloe. "It isn't anyone's birthday. Why are we eating so fancy? Oh, hey Dad. Whatcha doing here still?"

"I'm going to stick around the house today," Leroy replied mysteriously. "I have some repairs I want to do."

"Aunt Bernie, are you baking?" asked Grace.

"Why, yes I am," Bernie answered with a

twinkle in her voice. “Now, all of you find something to do after breakfast and leave us adults to adult.”

Bertram ran back and forth between them in search of handouts but also trying to figure out what was different. Humans had different vibrations and smells and today, from a dog’s point of view, everything was just a bit off.

“Wally, come join us in our room,” Lillian said. “We have to plan for today.”

Wally, closely followed by Bertram, appeared as though from nowhere as the girls settled on their beds.

“So here’s the thing,” began Lillian. “We have a spirit. I now know it’s a human — I know, I know, an alien would have been way cooler. Anyways, it’s trying to tell us something and somehow it has something to do with Chloe and Wally’s dad. That’s all we know.”

“Well, we also know it’s done some pretty weird tricks to get our attention,” added Grace. “And that it can move things, and apparently spell.”

“And it almost made itself visible and it tried to grab Lillian,” Chloe chimed in.

“And it’s a gentle soul,” added Wally.

All three girls swiveled their heads around to Wally. They'd completely forgotten he was even in the room. Chloe asked him, "How do you know?"

"Trust me, I know."

"Whatever, Wally, you weren't even there. You don't know anything."

Wally just smiled. He knew better than to argue with his sister.

"Okay," Chloe continued. "We need another backpack. Grab yours Lillian. We can stuff it with food and our phones and whatever else we need."

Wally grabbed his Indian Tobacco and put it in a pouch, which he placed in his pocket. Then they headed downstairs and outside to the porch. Bernie waved at them from the kitchen saying, "Okay you four, back in time for lunch! And stay out of the loft!"

As they were about to set off, Grace decided to leave the camera on the porch, as they didn't need it anymore to see the spirit. She tucked it under the cushion on the porch chair so her Aunt and Uncle wouldn't find it.

"Hey, before we go we're all going to smudge today," Lillian announced. "Even if you two feel weird about it. We need to go in that barn today with a good mind and an open spirit." Grace and Chloe rolled their eyes but they weren't about to argue with Lillian. Besides, they were starting to think that maybe, just maybe, Lillian and Wally knew more than they did.

Bertram was there too, but Wally shook his head.

"Stay," he commanded. "Today is not a day for you." Bertram whimpered but went inside when Wally opened the door for him.

Following the smudge, they bounded into the field towards the barn. They knew something was going to happen but they didn't know what. When they got to the barn door, Wally gave his pouch of tobacco to Lillian. She emptied it out on to the floor of the barn and prayed for help in whatever was about to happen. Then, holding hands, the four of them walked towards the loft stairs.

Chapter 19

Hearts and Minds Open

THEY ALL TOOK deep breaths. "Okay," said Lillian. "My Kokum told me a little bit about what's going on and we don't have to be afraid. We just have to open our hearts and mind and believe. Let's go."

They all stepped closer to the stairs. Once there, they didn't even think about how they were told not to go into the loft. Up they went. First Lillian, then Grace, then Chloe, and finally Wally. When they were all up the stairs they joined hands to give each other courage.

At first it seemed like nothing was going to happen. They waited to see some crazy stunts like things flying through the air, or swirling hay and straw, or huge gusts of wind, or even cold prickles down their backs, but what they felt was nothing. Absolutely nothing. Until at last they heard a very soft: "*Kwe.*" They looked at each other but they all shook their heads to say no it wasn't them that said it. They looked around and couldn't see anything, but then they noticed a figure standing in the corner, right by where the window that wasn't would have been. Grace and Chloe looked shocked and pale. Lillian and Wally replied with *"Kwe."*

They still couldn't see the figure clearly and none of them wanted to move closer. Grace and Chloe just dropped to the floor and sat quietly in shock. Lillian and Wally also sat down, but not out of fear. Lillian looked at Chloe and Grace.

"Hey now, don't be afraid," Lillian said. "We have to all believe and keep a good clear mind so we can get the spirit to fully appear. Okay, everyone think good thoughts. Open your mind and believe in the impossible. Let this spirit know we want to meet it. Don't be afraid."

They all took deep breaths and looked cautiously around the loft. It was very quiet and still until all four of them heard a faint swooshing sound and saw footsteps coming towards them.

Grace and Chloe started to panic but Lillian said, "Shhh, just wait."

Trembling, the girls remembered to believe, and slowly, ever so slowly, all four of them saw

The kids saw a girl about their same age.

the same thing. Walking towards them was a young girl, about their age, with long black hair and a long flowing dress, watching them closely.

“Wait a minute, you guys can actually see me now?” the girl asked. The spirit flapped her arms in front of her. “Wow, it’s about time! This has been exhausting.”

Suddenly, the whole mystical feeling in the loft disappeared and instead of a long flowing dress, the spirit girl was wearing a t-shirt, jeans, and running shoes with her hair in a ponytail.

“Hey!” shouted Grace “What’s going on? What are you doing? Who are you? Why are you messing with our heads?” The spirit shrugged.

“Mostly ’cause I’m bored, and ’cause I’ve waited so long for someone to see me.” She smiled. “Even when I started to get your attention you still weren’t looking hard enough, except you, Wally. *Kwe,* Wally nice to actually have you able to see me in the flesh...well, sorta.”

Grace and Chloe stared at Wally. “You know her?” Chloe said.

“Not exactly,” said Wally. “I’ve never seen her, but I’ve heard her and kinda felt her.”

“Why didn’t you tell me, or Mom and Dad?” asked Chloe.

"Seriously? Think about it, would any of you have listened to me?"

Chloe shamefully lowered her head. "Well… No."

"Exactly. Besides, the messages aren't for me. She wanted to talk to you, Chloe, but you weren't open to believing. When Lillian showed up, she knew Lillian was a believer and this was her chance to communicate. There's one more day before she returns to the spirit world for good. That's why today is so important."

"Hey, remember me? The spirit girl? I'm over here. Man, it's hard to keep you guys focused."

All four stood and stared at her, still trying to take in the fact that she really existed. "Oh, yeah, there's your backpack and stuff. Except for the candy. For some reason I was able to eat those gummys and boy were they good."

Lillian looked her directly in the eye. "You have one day left here before you go back to the spirit world, right? So, who are you and why are you still here?"

With those words the girl's expression became very serious and sad.

"My name is Cheyenne," she said. "I'm 11 years old and I'm here with a message for Leroy."

"Well, why can't you just tell him yourself?" mumbled Chloe.

"Because he stopped believing in everything a long time ago. Adults aren't as connected to the spirit world as kids are, and I need to tell someone he'll listen to."

"Why didn't you just tell me?" asked Chloe, "or Wally?"

"Do you seriously think he would have listened to either of you?"

"Good point," Chloe agreed, reluctant. "But, why Lillian?"

"Why not?" was the response. "She was here and open to believing. She got you to believe too. Thank you, all of you. It's nice to finally be able to talk to someone of this world."

Cheyenne gave a small smile and turned to Lillian.

"Lillian, I need to speak with you alone, and after, you can share what I say."

Cheyenne and Lillian went over to the corner where Cheyenne had appeared from. Chloe, Grace, and Wally watched them speak together bent head-to-head. They saw Lillian look up in surprise and shock, while Cheyenne's face turned very sad. They continued talking for a while, then they watched Lillian fall to the ground crying and weeping inconsolably. They saw Cheyenne wrap her arms around her until Lillian smiled and nodded. Finally they came back.

"Okay, Lillian. It's up to you now. I don't know why I was gifted with a visit to this world, but *Mishomis* gave me a time limit and today's the day. Remember in your prayers to give him thanks and—"

Suddenly, they were interrupted by a loud shout at the bottom of the stairs. They had been so intently listening to Cheyenne that they hadn't heard Chloe's parents enter the barn.

"What in the devil are you four doing up in the loft?!" shouted Leroy. "Get down this minute!" All of them were too shocked to move even an inch.

"I said, get down now! Have you all gone deaf? Right now!" Still, no one moved. Leroy grabbed at the stairs and scurried up them followed by Bernie who looked very disappointed with the children. The four of them looked at Cheyenne, who frowned, and back at Leroy and Bernie. Leroy still looked furious and Bernie still looked sad and disappointed. Neither of them looked at Cheyenne. Finally, Chloe courageously said: “Can’t you see anything, Dad? Wally make him see! Lillian?” They both sadly shook their heads at her.

“See what?” said Bernie. “Don’t try to distract us from the fact that you’re up here!”

“Who’s Cheyenne?” asked Lillian looking directly at Leroy and Bernie.

Chloe and Wally swung their gaze to their parents, asking, “Yes, who is she?”

With that sentence, Leroy went completely still and began to shake. Bernie became ashen, as if she were about to pass out.

“Who told you about Cheyenne?” Leroy said, much quieter now. “What’s she got to do with you being up here?”

Lillian looked at Cheyenne.

“Tell him what I told you,” she said. “Remember, he can’t see me. I might be able to make him feel something though, or do some of those parlour tricks you liked.”

Lillian approached Leroy.

“It’s okay. I know who Cheyenne was. I know she was your little sister.”

Chloe and Wally gasped. Even Wally didn’t know this. Lillian continued.

“I know you blame yourself and your mom

for her death, but… Cheyenne says to stop it right now." Lillian looked to Cheyenne for reassurance and she nodded her head for Lillian to keep going. "She said, 'Leroy, it's time for your kids to know about their Aunt, and by the way she thinks Chloe and Wally grew into pretty cool kids.'" Cheyenne grinned at Chloe and Wally, who stared at her in shock. "Our Auntie??!!" They shouted together.

Leroy at this point had dropped to his knees in shock. "But how could you know?" he murmured. "Bernie? This isn't funny."

"I've never said anything to anyone," she replied.

Again, Lillian looked at Cheyenne, who nodded. "Cheyenne says you used to call her 'pickle face' because she would eat as many pickles as she could just to get that scrunched up face from the sour taste."

With that, Leroy started to cry and Bernie put her arms around him. Even she hadn't known about that. Chloe and Wally felt weird because they'd never seen their dad cry before. Grace just felt strange and out of place.

"Lillian," Cheyenne said. "I'm going to try and get my brother to feel me. Then tell him the rest of the story."

Cheyenne stood beside her brother and put her hands on his shoulders. She had seen this on so many TV shows and movies while she was alive, and she sure hoped it worked for real. At first it didn't seem to have any effect, but then Leroy's shoulders stopped heaving and he got a strange look on his face.

"Okay," said Lillian, allowing Cheyenne's words to flow through her, "Cheyenne says to stop being mad at your mom, and stop being mad at yourself. She says she slipped and fell on those rocks. It was no one's fault but hers. Your mom was right in telling you to watch her. You did watch her, and you yelled at her to get away from the rocks but she wouldn't listen and she says she's sorry."

Cheyenne continued her explanation, through Lillian. "If she'd listened she would still be here today and you wouldn't have wasted time hating yourself and blaming your mom. Your mom and your other sister, Grace's mom, carry that guilt too, and you don't help it by cutting her out of your life and your family's life and turning your back on the old ways. Cheyenne says she's sorry she drowned on your watch, but it was her own fault and nobody else's. She said it's okay to grieve her but don't stay in that spot. Your mother and your wife and your kids need you." Lillian dropped her eyes for a moment but continued, speaking Cheyenne's exact words, "Celebrate my life. It was good and filled with love. Remember, I was an adventurous 11-year-old kid with a mind of my own."

Lillian stopped and looked at Cheyenne for direction. She needed a rest.

Cheyenne still stood with her hands on her brother's shoulder. "Hey, I think he feels it," she said. "It's just like in the movies." The four kids started to giggle. Leroy and Bernie looked at them sternly.

"Oh, we're not laughing at you, Dad," Chloe said. "Cheyenne's touching your shoulders and says it's just like in the movies. Can you really feel it?"

Leroy looked back and forth at his shoulders, smiling. "Tell Cheyenne it's working, I feel her hands."

"She can hear you, Dad," Wally said. "You and Mom can't see or hear her but she hears and sees you."

Cheyenne waved at Lillian to get her attention.

“I have to leave soon,” said Cheyenne. “I can feel the pull to the spirit world. Tell my brother the rest when I leave and remind him to give thanks to *Mishomis* for giving us the gift of this visit. It won’t happen again and tell him I am happy. *Miigwech*, Lillian.”

Cheyenne stepped away from Leroy to give Lillian a big hug, which only the other children could see. Then, she hugged her niece Chloe and nephew Wally, and told them to listen to their parents. Finally, she hugged her niece Grace and thanked her for helping them. All the parents could see was the slightest hint of a weight on their shoulders.

“Hey, what’s going on up there,” came a voice from the barn door. “A party without us?”

Everyone looked down the stairs and there, grinning up at them, were two Kokums and Lillian’s Auntie.

“What are you doing here?!” screamed Lillian.

“This is the surprise,” said Bernie. “We invited your Auntie and Kokum for a visit and they brought Chloe, Wally, and Grace’s Kokum with them too, from the Rez.”

Chloe’s Kokum saw the look on Leroy’s face

and suddenly grew very quiet. Cheyenne saw her mother looking up as she was looking down.

"Oh, Momma," she said. "I wish you could see me. I wish I could hug you. But I'm leaving now, I feel it. I'm sorry I didn't listen to Leroy that day. I love you, and I'm okay here Momma. Honest."

Chloe's Kokum, Cheyenne's mother, nodded and said, "It's alright, my daughter. I feel you and I hear you. I love you too."

With those words, Cheyenne faded from the kids' sight. They could still hear her but only slightly. "Remember all I told you, Lillian," and then she was gone.

Chapter 20

Cheyenne's Old Camera

EVERYONE FELT IT, even the adults. The emptiness. The quiet. Everyone took a moment to gather their thoughts. Leroy and Bernie were still in shock over everything that happened and the two Kokums and Auntie knew they had missed most of it, but witnessed part of a very special moment. At last, Lillian's Kokum brought them all back into focus.

"Come down now," said Kokum. "We have things to discuss and things to do."

Lillian grabbed the backpack that they had left there the previous day and they all cautiously went down the stairs. Lillian ran into Auntie's arms and then Kokum's arms. "I missed you so much," she cried. "I have so much more to tell you, and some things still need to be done today."

Everyone slowly walked back to the house lost in thought. Leroy had his arm around his mother and was softly sobbing. Bernie walked behind, giving them their time together. Lillian walked between her Kokum and Auntie, and Wally tailed with Bertram, who had run out of the house after Bernie and Leroy. Grace and Chloe were both still in awe of everything.

“Kokum, there is more,” said Lillian a short while later.

“Yes, I know, granddaughter.”

Everyone was sitting together on the porch enjoying the afternoon together. Leroy felt something under his pillow and pulled out the camera that Grace had hidden there. “What in the world?” he exclaimed as he saw what it was. “This is Cheyenne’s old camera.”

“I gave that camera to Cheyenne for her birthday,” said Chloe’s Kokum. “Where could that have come from?”

“I found it in the barn,” said Chloe. “That’s how this whole adventure started.”

The four kids proceeded to tell the adults the entire story.

“Did you know there are still pictures on here?” Leroy asked when they were done. They all looked at each other, amazed. They’d never thought of there being any other pictures on it, or even trying anything with the camera except looking through the lens and at the screen. They had only looked at the five pictures they took of the barn and it never crossed their minds to go beyond that. Leroy pulled out the tiny storage card that was inside of it. "Follow me, my computer has a slot for these old cards."

Everyone gathered around the computer and looked at the pictures of Cheyenne and Leroy and Grace's mom Sandra when they were young. They all looked happy. Leroy's mother smiled.

"That is how I will always remember you," she said. "Happy."

"There is more I have to tell you," remembered Lillian. "Cheyenne said to have a feast today, but I know there isn't time, so…"

"There is time," Kokum said. "I had a dream, Lillian, and we have been preparing for this feast for several days. We just didn't know why. We know it's a feast for two, but we don't know who the second person is. Perhaps you can tell us now."

Lillian looked shyly at everyone. "Don't be afraid," her Kokum said. "You are safe here."

Lillian started slowly.

"Well, Cheyenne told me more, and this did

involve me. Cheyenne said she met my little sister, the one I've been missing ever since I've been in foster care. She said my little sister is happy with *Mishomis*. She said her body lies under a beautiful big tree and that she doesn't want anyone to move her bones. She's happy there. She asked for a feast and said the feast would make her happy."

Everyone shed some tears for the little girl who wasn't with them anymore. When the tears were finished flowing, Leroy's mother clapped her hands together and said, "Now, unload the coolers with all the food. Tonight we honour our loved ones and feast."

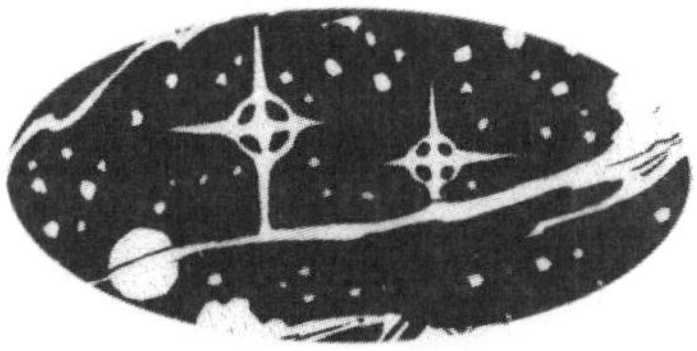

After everyone had eaten, Lillian and Leroy took plates of food that had been made up for their family members who had passed, and walked them out to the bush to leave for the spirits. There was no longer a window or light in the barn, but both of them were sure they saw two bright new stars in the sky.

Anishinaabek Words

Kokum taught us these words:

Miigwech

Kokum says to say *miigwech* every day.
We say *miigwech* to the Creator ***Mishomis***
for the great gifts that he has given us.

Aniin

A way to say hello.

Kwe

A less-formal way to say hello.

Kokum or ***Kokomis***

Grandmother....(our favourite).

Wewiibitaan

Hurry up.

Wabi, nondam

See and hear.

Kisagin

I love you.

Acknowledgements

Above all I want to acknowledge all of our little ones in the Spirit World. Know that you were loved and are loved.

I'd like to thank everyone in my amazing family and in my circle of friends for their continued understanding and support.

To Dave Nicholson the incredibly talented illustrator for this book as always you breathe life into my stories. *Miigwech.*

Special thanks to my advance readers Chloe and Grace Wyville, Leo Massi, Linda Pattison, Robin Decontie, and Sandy Herkimer.

The book would not be here in front of you without the ever-helpful input from Durvile & UpRoute Books. This includes the continuous encouragement, input, and suggestions from publisher Lorene Shyba and series editor Raymond Yakeleya, along with amazing editorial and proofing help from Maddy Shyba and Meghan Whitsitt.

A very sincere thanks ever so much.

—Lynda Partridge, 2022

Photo: Jordyn Lipsett

About the Author, Lynda Partridge

Lynda Partridge is a member of the Algonquins of Pikwakanagan First Nation. She is a mother, a grandmother, a wife, an auntie, and a sister. She grew up in the child welfare system and spent her childhood in numerous non-Indigenous foster homes. At a later age she obtained an honours Bachelor of Social Work (Native Human Services), followed by a Masters of Social Work Degree. It was while obtaining her undergraduate degree that she found her birth family and reconnected to her Indigenous culture. This experience led her to the field of Indigenous child welfare.

About the Illustrator, Dave Nicholson

Dave Nicholson was born in Muskoka, Ontario and now lives on Gabriola Island, British Columbia. Dave established himself as an award-winning tattoo artist early in life and he has since branched into wide-ranging and diverse mediums. He holds a lifelong interest in graphic storytelling. Largely self-taught, and educated, this is his debut as a kid's book illustrator. He considers it a great honour to illustrate this story for his Auntie Lynda.